Stories for Christmas

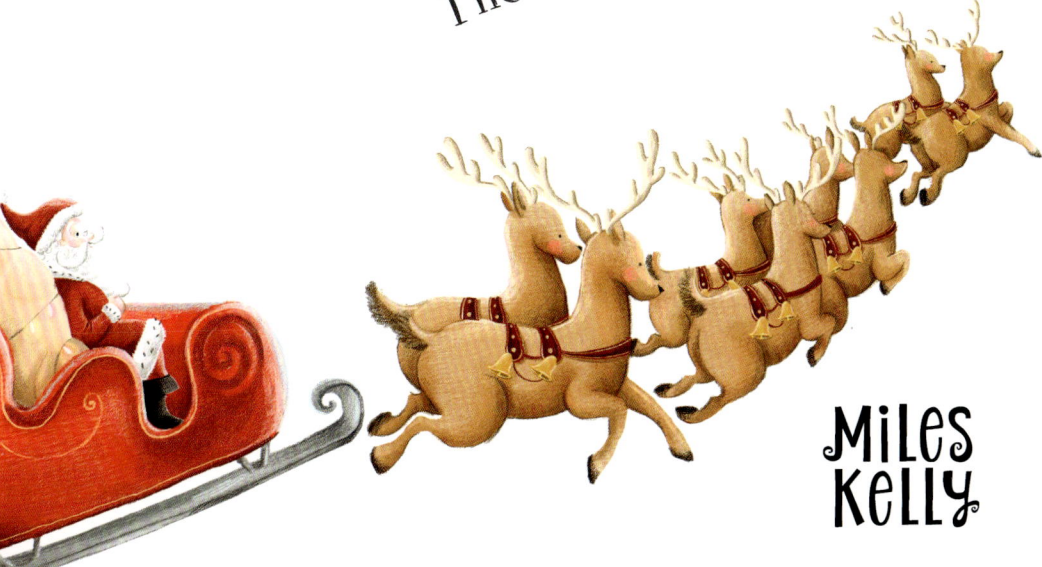

MILES KELLY

First published in 2021 by Miles Kelly Publishing Ltd
Harding's Barn, Bardfield End Green, Thaxted, Essex, CM6 3PX, UK

2 4 6 8 10 9 7 5 3 1

Publishing Director Belinda Gallagher
Creative Director Jo Cowan
Editorial Director Rosie Neave
Senior Editors Fran Bromage, Amy Johnson
Cover Designer Jo Cowan
Design Manager Joe Jones
Senior Designer Emily Stalley
Image Manager Liberty Newton
Production Controller Jennifer Brunwin
Reprographics Stephan Davis
Assets Lorraine King

ISBN 978-1-78989-311-3

Printed in China

British Library Cataloguing-in-Publication Data
A catalogue record for this book is available from the British Library

ACKNOWLEDGEMENTS
The publishers would like to thank the following artists who have contributed to this book:
The Bright Agency: Rosie Butcher (The Night Before Christmas), Sue Reeves (cover)
Advocate Art: Jean Claude (The Nutcracker) and Ela Smietanka (The Snow Queen)
Lemonade Illustration Agency: Luis Filella (The Twelve Days of Christmas)

Made with paper from a sustainable forest

www.mileskelly.net

The Night Before Christmas

'Twas the night before Christmas,
when all through the house
Not a creature was stirring,
not even a mouse.

The stockings were hung
by the chimney with care,
In hopes that St Nicholas
soon would be there.

5

When out on the lawn
there arose such a clatter,
I sprang from the bed
to see what was the matter.

6

Away to the window
I flew like a flash,
Tore open the shutters
and threw up the sash.

The moon on the breast
of the new-fallen snow,
Gave the lustre of midday
to objects below.

When, what to my
wondering eyes should appear,
But a miniature sleigh,
and eight tiny reindeer.

9

With a little old driver,
so lively and quick,
I knew in a moment
it must be St Nick.

10

More rapid than eagles
his coursers they came,
And he whistled, and shouted,
and called them by name!

"Now, Dasher! Now, Dancer!
Now, Prancer and Vixen!
On, Comet! On, Cupid!
On, Donner and Blitzen!

To the top of the porch!
To the top of the wall!
Now dash away! Dash away!
Dash away all!"

As dry leaves that before
the wild hurricane fly,
When they meet with an
obstacle, mount to the sky.

So up to the house-top
the coursers they flew,
With the sleigh full of toys,
and St Nicholas too.

And then, in a twinkling,
I heard on the roof
The prancing and pawing
of each little hoof.

As I drew in my head,
and was turning around,
Down the chimney St Nicholas
came with a bound.

He was dressed all in fur,
from his head to his foot,
And his clothes were all
tarnished with ashes and soot.

14

A bundle of toys
he had flung on his back,
And he looked like a peddler,
just opening his pack.

His eyes – how they twinkled!
His dimples how merry!
His cheeks were like roses,
his nose like a cherry!

His droll little mouth
was drawn up like a bow,
And the beard of his chin
was as white as the snow.

The stump of a pipe
he held tight in his teeth,
And the smoke it encircled
his head like a wreath.

He had a broad face
and a little round belly,
That shook when he laughed,
like a bowlful of jelly!

He was chubby and plump,
a right jolly old elf,
And I laughed when I saw him,
in spite of myself!

A wink of his eye
and a twist of his head,
Soon gave me to know
I had nothing to dread.

19

He spoke not a word,
but went straight to his work,
And filled all the stockings,
then turned with a jerk.

And laying his finger
aside of his nose,
And giving a nod,
up the chimney he rose!

He sprang to his sleigh,
to his team gave a whistle,
And away they all flew
like the down of a thistle.

23

But I heard him exclaim, 'ere he drove out of sight

"Happy Christmas to all, and to all a good night!"

The Nutcracker

It was Christmas
Eve, and snow was
falling softly outside.
Clara thought it
looked **magical.**

26

Inside, the party was in full swing. Clara's little brother Franz was running around the **twinkling** Christmas tree.

Clara spotted her godfather and ran to greet him. He always brought exciting presents.

Clara's present was very unusual and very special.
It was a **nutcracker.**

It was painted to look like a smart
toy soldier.

You put a nut in its mouth and pressed a lever. But then Franz tried to crack a walnut that was too big.

CRACK!

The nutcracker's jaw snapped!
"I'll mend him in the morning,"
promised Clara's godfather.

At bedtime, Clara put the **nutcracker** under the tree with the other toys and went to bed. But she couldn't sleep.

So Clara got out of bed and crept downstairs. She picked up the nutcracker and snuggled down next to the Christmas tree. Her eyes began to close.

As the clock struck **midnight**, Clara woke to find she had shrunk to the size of a doll. The **Nutcracker** stood before her. He smiled at Clara, and bowed.

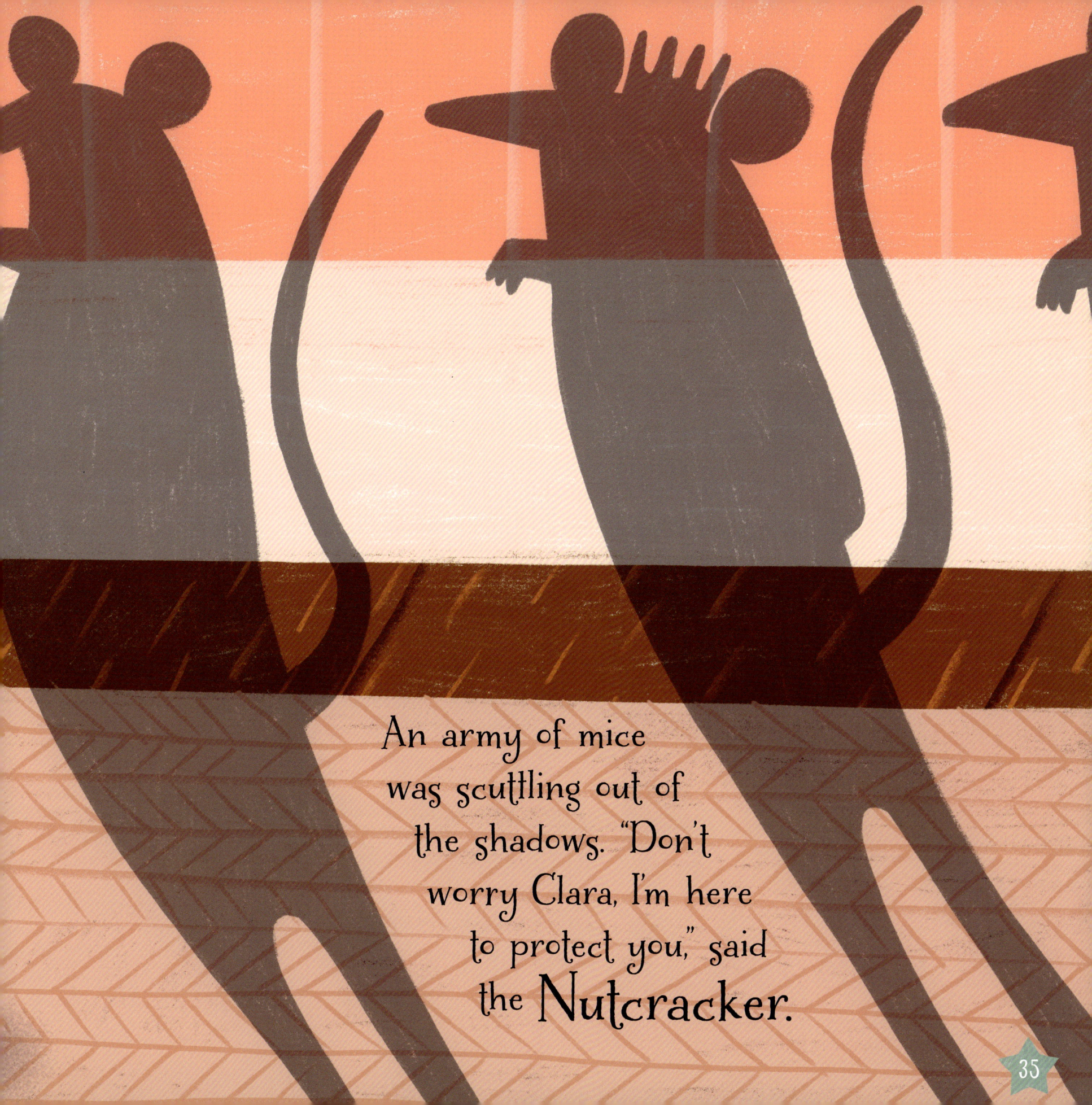

An army of mice
was scuttling out of
the shadows. "Don't
worry Clara, I'm here
to protect you," said
the Nutcracker.

The toy soldiers and the **Nutcracker** drew their swords.

With a loud squeak, the **Mouse King** and his army charged.

Clara wanted to help.
She took off her slipper
and **threw it** at
the Mouse King.

The Mouse King fell to the ground and all the other mice fled.

"You have broken the Mouse King's spell," said the Nutcracker. "I am a prince who has been trapped as a toy for years."

He gave Clara the Mouse King's crown.

"We must celebrate!" cried the **prince**. A magical sleigh appeared at once, and Clara's nightdress became **a beautiful ballgown.**

The **prince** and Clara flew through the snowy night in the sleigh until they reached the **Land of Sweets.**

"Welcome to Marzipan Palace!"
They were met by a beautiful
Sugar Plum Fairy.

The Prince told her
what Clara had done.
"We will have a banquet to
say thanks," said the fairy.

43

Tables of **beautiful** food appeared, with treats from all over the world.

Dancers from every country
whirled and **pranced.**
Clara was entranced.

Clara curled up in her chair to watch. It was **enchanting.**

Last of all, the prince and the **Sugar Plum Fairy** performed a **magnificent waltz.**

Slowly, Clara's eyes began to close.

When Clara awoke she was at home once more.

Her nutcracker was lying in her arms, and his jaw looked like new. But now he was **smiling**.

The Snow Queen

Gerda and Kay lived next door to each other, and were the best of friends.

"Hello Kay!"

The two told each other everything, and loved playing outside together.

On winter evenings they would sit by the fire, listening to Gerda's grandma telling stories. They loved the one about the

Snow Queen.

"The **Snow Queen** lives in a huge palace
of ice," said Grandma. "Her enchantments chill
your heart, so you forget who you are."

That night, Kay couldn't sleep. He opened his window and gazed out at the icy street.

Just at that moment, the
Snow Queen threw down
a shard of enchanted ice.
It captured Kay's heart.

55

The next day, Kay shouted at his mother and didn't play nicely with anyone.

56

Kay was even **mean** to Gerda. The Snow Queen's **cold magic** was chilling his heart.

One morning Kay was playing
alone when a **sparkling**
sleigh appeared over the hill.

The Snow Queen had
come to take Kay away.

When Gerda noticed **Kay was gone** she looked everywhere. But Kay was nowhere to be found.

Gerda felt certain the **Snow Queen** had stolen Kay. So, she left the village to **search** for him.

After many miles,
Gerda met a **raven**.
"I've seen your friend,"
said the raven. "He's
at the **Snow**
Queen's palace."

Gerda followed the path the raven pointed to. It led through a forest where some **robbers** lived.

The **robbers** locked Gerda in
their barn. One of the robbers
had a daughter, and Gerda told
her about her **search** for Kay.

63

The robber's daughter helped
Gerda **escape** so she could
continue her journey.

The girl gave Gerda a **reindeer** to ride, and a warm cloak to wear.

"My reindeer will know the way," said the girl.

The reindeer ran through **overgrown woods** and climbed steep, snowy slopes for many days.

At last, frozen and exhausted, Gerda arrived at the Snow Queen's **ice palace**.

Gerda opened the **door** and peeped in. Kay was sitting on the **frozen floor.**

The **Snow Queen** was near, so Gerda whispered Kay's name, but Kay didn't seem to recognize her at all!

69

As soon as the Snow Queen left the room, Gerda ran to Kay. But Kay wouldn't, or couldn't, move. Gerda felt helpless.

Gerda started to cry, and her tears melted the ice in Kay's heart. Kay looked at Gerda. "I remember you," he said.

71

Their friendship made the sun shine. The ice palace melted and the Snow Queen fled. Flowers bloomed and a path showed Gerda and Kay the way home.

The Twelve Days of Christmas

On the **first day** of Christmas my true love gave to me,

a partridge in a pear tree.

On the **second day**
of Christmas my true
love gave to me,

two turtle doves

and a partridge
in a pear tree.

On the **third day** of Christmas
my true love gave to me,

three French hens,

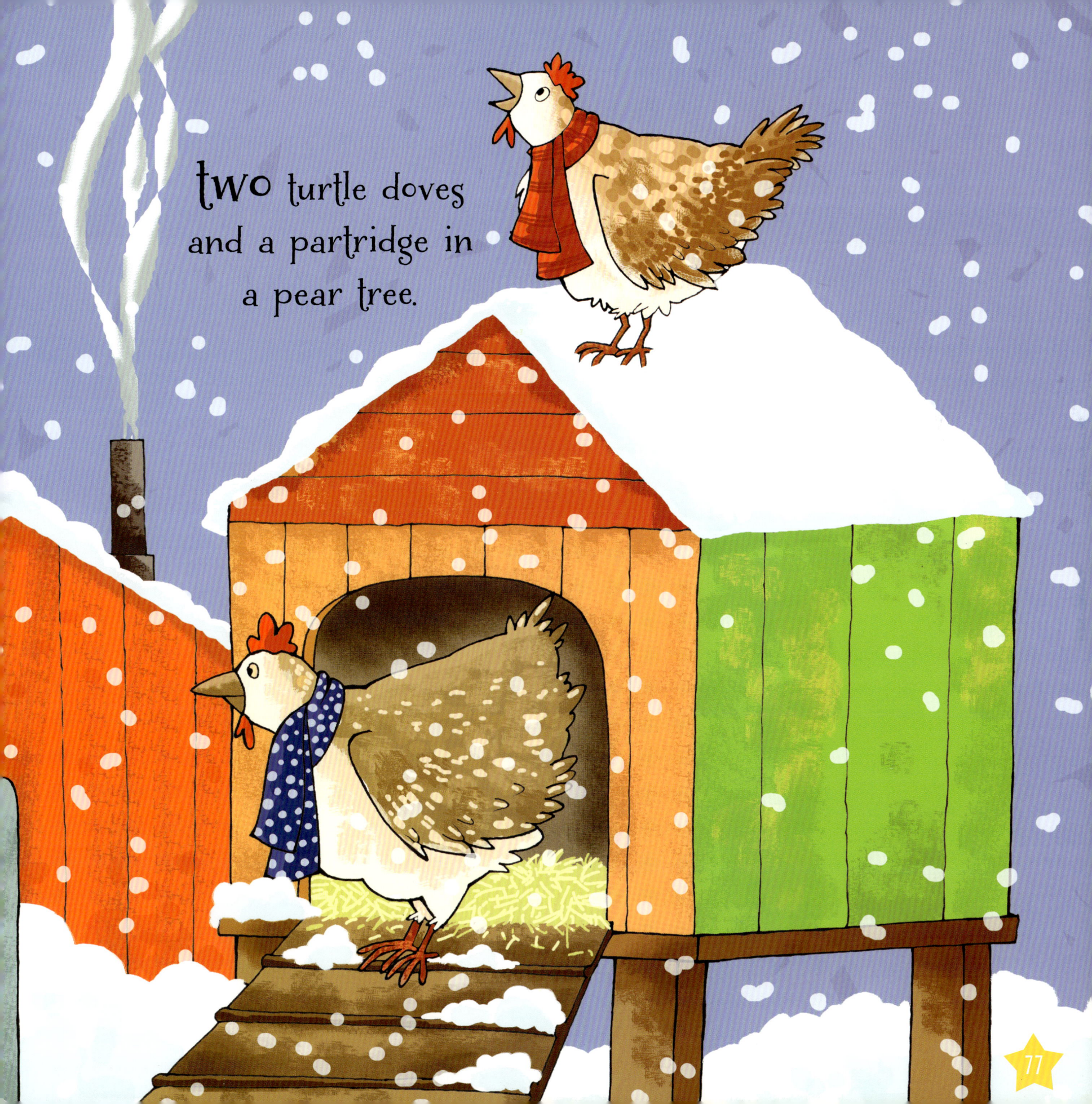

two turtle doves
and a partridge in
a pear tree.

77

On the **fourth day** of Christmas
my true love gave to me,

four calling birds,

78

three French hens,
two turtle doves
and a partridge in
a pear tree.

79

On the **fifth day** of Christmas
my true love gave to me,

five gold rings,

four calling birds, three French hens,
two turtle doves and
a partridge in a pear tree.

On the **sixth** day of Christmas
my true love gave to me,

six geese a-laying,

five gold rings, four calling birds,
three French hens, two turtle doves
and a partridge in a pear tree.

On the **seventh** day of Christmas
my true love gave to me,

seven swans
a-swimming,

six geese a-laying, five gold rings,
four calling birds, three French hens,
two turtle doves and a
partridge in a pear tree.

85

On the **eighth** day of Christmas
my true love gave to me,

eight maids a-milking,

seven swans a-swimming,
six geese a-laying,
five gold rings, **four** calling birds,
three French hens, **two** turtle doves
and a partridge in a pear tree.

87

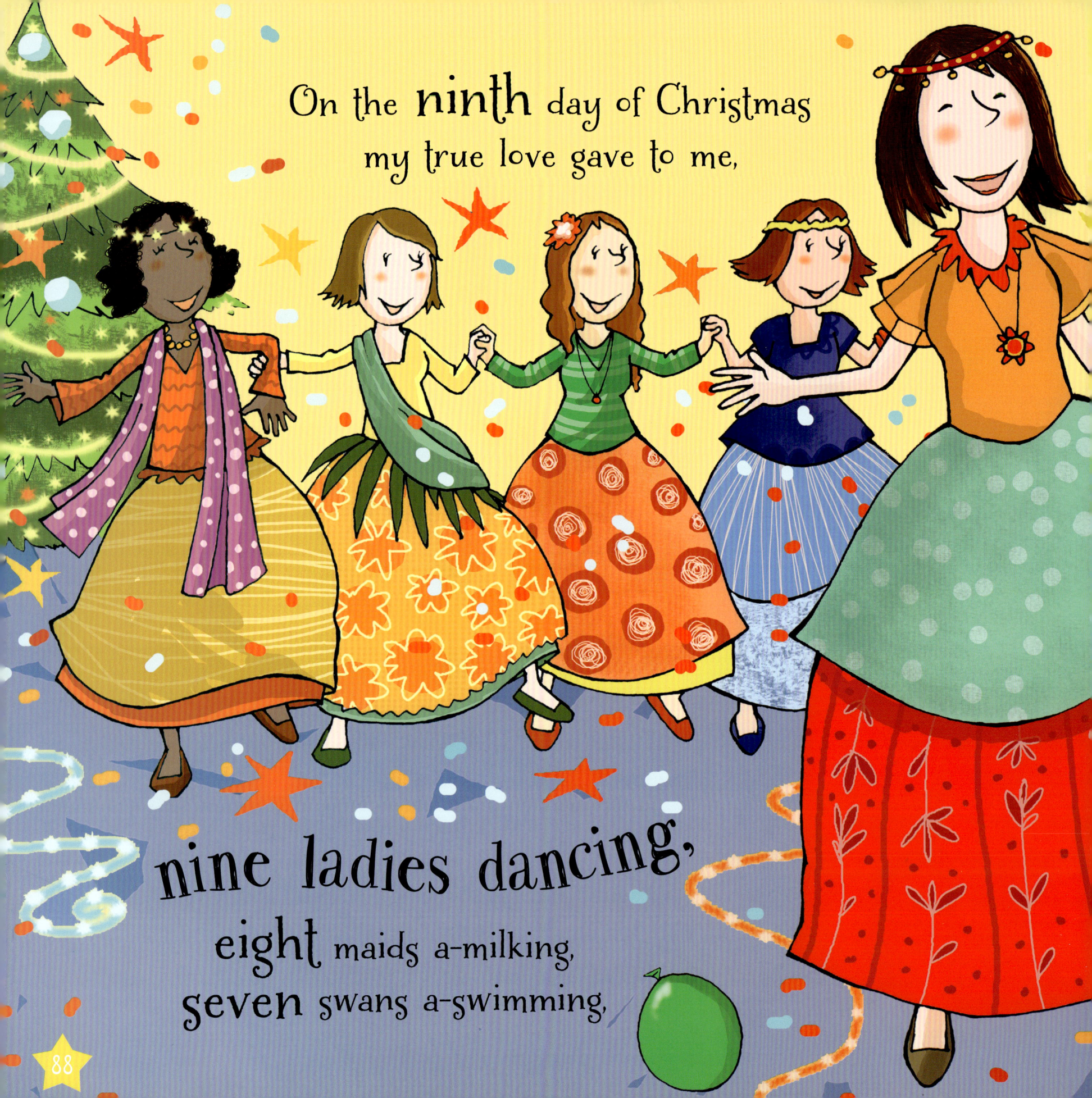

six geese a-laying, five gold rings,
four calling birds, three French hens,

two turtle doves
and a partridge in a pear tree.

On the **tenth** day of Christmas
my true love gave to me,

**ten lords
a-leaping,**

nine ladies dancing,
eight maids a-milking,

seven swans a-swimming,
six geese a-laying,
five gold rings, four calling birds,
three French hens, two turtle doves
and a partridge in a pear tree.

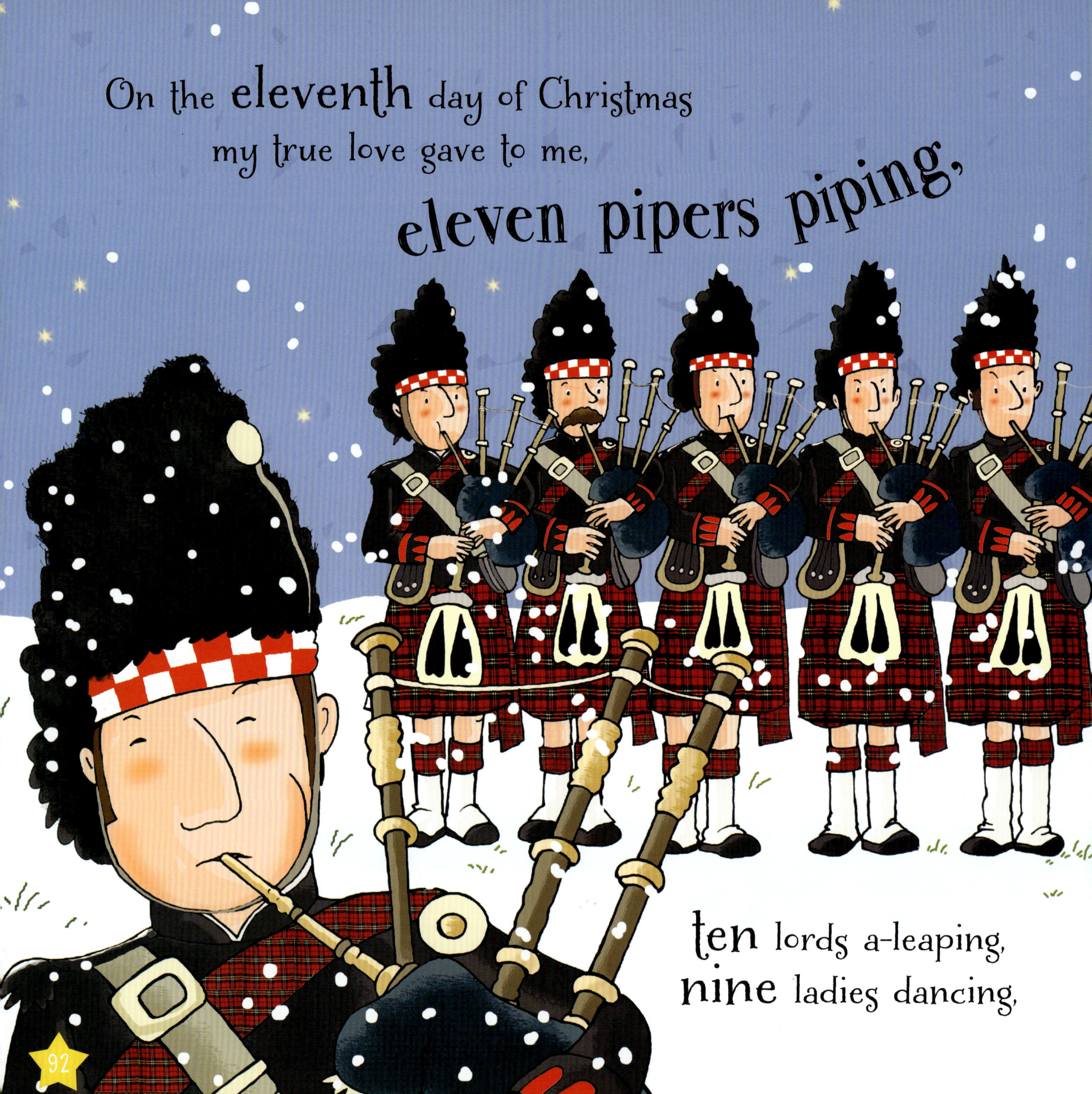

eight maids a-milking, seven swans a-swimming,
six geese a-laying, five gold rings,
four calling birds, three French hens,
two turtle doves and a partridge in a pear tree.

93

On the **twelfth** day of Christmas
my true love gave to me,
twelve drummers drumming,

eleven pipers piping,
ten lords a-leaping,
nine ladies dancing,
eight maids a-milking,
seven swans a-swimming,

six geese a-laying, five gold rings, four calling birds,
three French hens, two turtle doves
and a partridge in a pear tree.

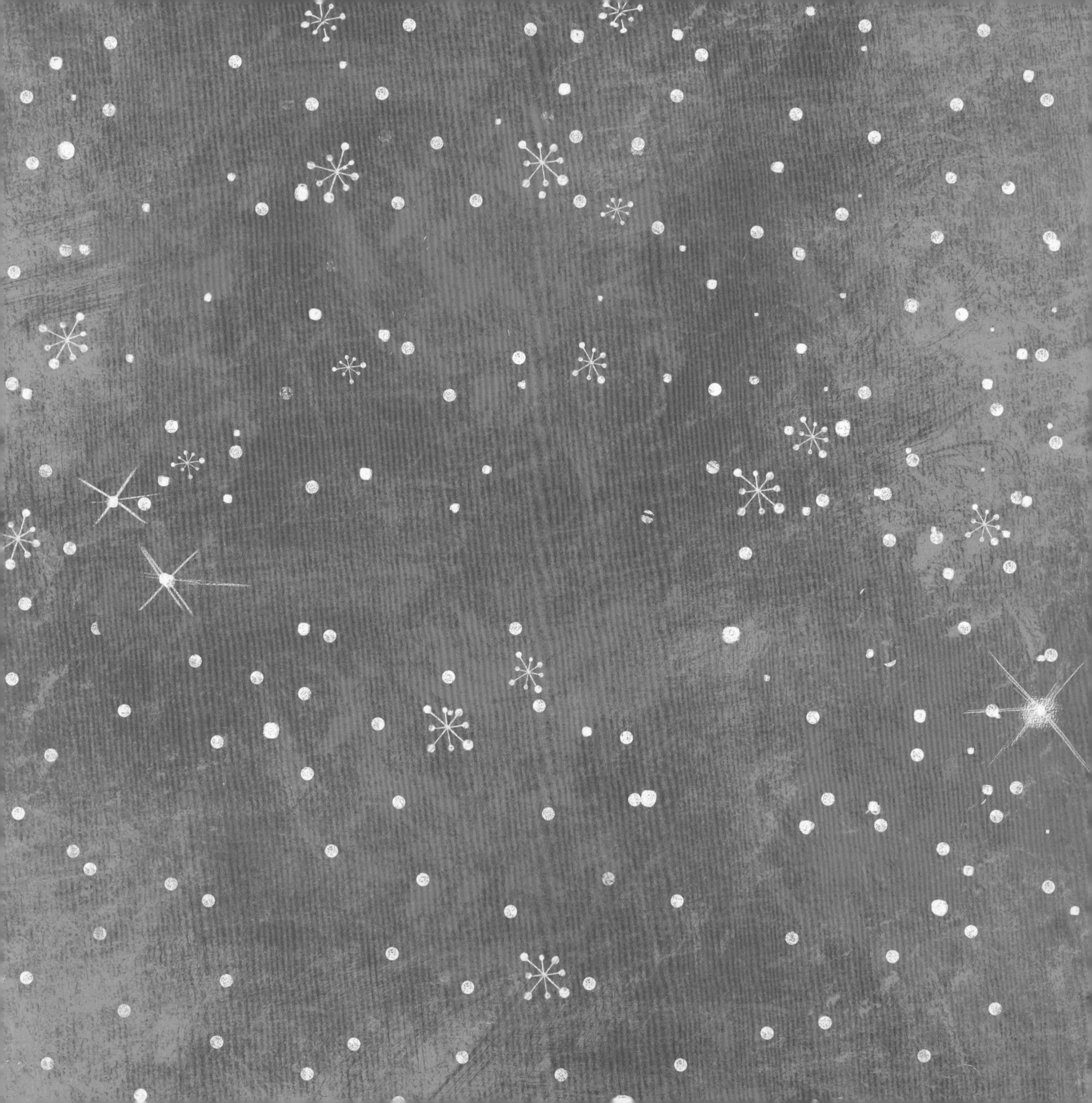